"I'm No Ordinary Chicken!" written by Roy and Doris Nichols.
Copyright © 1987 by Sweet Publishing, Fort Worth, TX 76137.

Illustrations originally published in "Die Henne Ottokar" with
story by Edith Schreiber-Wicke. Illustrations by Paul Mangold.
Copyright © 1986 by Paul Mangold.

Library of Congress Catalog Card Number 87-42785
ISBN 0-8344-0143-6

Cover design: Koechel/Peterson Design, Mpls., MN

10 9 8 7 6 5 4 3 2 1

I'm No Ordinary Chicken!

By

ROY *and* **DORIS NICHOLS**

Illustrated by

PAUL MANGOLD

Sweet Publishing

3934 Sandshell, Ft. Worth, TX 76137

"Hattie, you're going to get into trouble again," said Fiddlefoot.

"Not me! I'm too smart."

"That's what you said last time, and the fox nearly had you for lunch. Why can't you be happy here? God has given us this beautiful meadow. This old tree is cool and pleasant and is a safe place to sleep. Farmer Schultz gives us food and water. What more could you want?"

"Dull! Dull! Dull!" said Hattie. "Nothing interesting ever happens here. Besides, I want to know what's in Farmer Yoder's big barn."

"You'd better stay away from there," said Fiddlefoot. "Farmer Yoder isn't as loving and kind as Farmer Schultz."

"She won't listen to anyone, not even her friends," said Goldilegs. "Let her find out for herself."

"You're nothing but a bunch of silly country hens," said Hattie as she flew down from the tree. "I'm no ordinary chicken. I'm braver than you are. I'm smarter than you are. I'm prettier than you are, and . . .

I can lay better eggs than you, too!" And with that, Hattie laid a pretty white egg in the grass. Then, without even saying good-bye to her friends, she strutted off to see what she could find.

As she walked along, she sang . . .

"I'm a very fine hen, a smart little hen.
No ordinary hen am I.
Let the other hens talk. I won't give a squawk!
I'm telling this dull place good-bye."

Soon Hattie began to feel hungry. She thought about the corn Farmer Schultz fed her. She thought about the delicious worms in the meadow. "I'm a very smart hen. I'll find something better than corn to eat. I'll find bigger and better worms, too."

Nearby two farmers were talking. "Perhaps they will give me some food," she thought. Just as she walked up to the men, she saw something on the ground. . . .

"A great big, long, brown, juicy worm," thought Hattie.
"It's the longest worm I've ever seen. I knew a smart
hen like me could find something to
eat." But just as she started to
gobble it up . . .

the worm took a big jump. And away it went, chasing after the farmer.

"This is the strangest worm I've ever seen," clucked Hattie. "It doesn't act at all like the worms in the meadow. I must catch it and take it home with me. Then the other hens will see what a wonderful worm catcher I am."

But no matter how fast Hattie ran, the worm
kept ahead of her jumping down the road. At
last, Hattie grew tired. "Well! I certainly don't
want to spend the whole day chasing a silly
worm." She was hot and her short little legs
would carry her no farther.

As Hattie lay down in the grass to rest, over the hill came a lady in a green dress.

It was Farmer Yoder's wife. She had been watching Hattie. "I think that silly chicken belongs to Farmer Schultz," the lady said to herself. "She's more trouble than she's worth, but if I don't catch her, something terrible might happen to her."

She picked up the tired little hen and tucked her under her arm. "If you were my hen, I'd make you into chicken soup. Then you wouldn't run away and get into trouble," said Mrs. Yoder as she held on to one of Hattie's fat legs.

Hattie was frightened. She flapped her wings. She squawked and kicked, but Farmer Yoder's wife held her tightly. The next thing Hattie knew, the lady opened the door to the big barn and tossed her inside.

"Get off me, you clumsy hen."

"Where did you come from?"

"What are you doing here? You're not from this farm."

Every hen in the barn was talking at once, and none of them were glad to see her.

"Where am I?" asked Hattie when things had quieted down.

A hen named Eggalina said, "You're in Farmer Yoder's hen house, and I must say, you have no business here at all! We're prize-winning egg layers, and you're just an ordinary country chicken. How did you get here anyway?"

The proud, cross words made Hattie feel awful.
"Well, I was out for a walk in the grass when I saw this worm. . . ."

"Grass? What's that?" asked one hen.

"Worm? What's a worm?" asked another.

"Why would you go for a walk?" asked a third.

No matter how hard Hattie tried to explain, the hens didn't understand.

"That sounds terrible," said Eggalina when she heard about worms. "We would never eat anything like that. And we're much too busy laying eggs to do foolish things like taking a walk," added a squawky voice. "You really should leave. You're just a silly country hen, and you don't belong here."

"How rude!" thought Hattie. "These hens don't know anything, but they think they're so smart. I'm glad I'm not like…" Hattie started to say "THEM." But she stopped. "I AM like them! I said the same unkind things to my friends, my very best friends. If only I could get out of this awful place, I'd go back and tell them how sorry I am." She was sad and very frightened.

Hattie was still sitting with her head down when Farmer Yoder opened the door. Standing next to him was Farmer Schultz. "There she is, just as my wife told you," Farmer Yoder said. "Why do you keep such a silly chicken? She doesn't lay as many eggs as my hens. And she's always getting into trouble. If she were my hen, I'd sell her or make her into chicken soup."

"Oh, we couldn't do that!" said Farmer Schultz. "It's true; she sometimes gets into trouble and does foolish things. But we still love her. Thank you for taking care of her. Perhaps she's learned her lesson this time."

As Farmer Schultz walked down the road back to the farm, Hattie followed along behind thinking about what she had heard. Farmer Schultz wasn't mad at her. He had even said they loved her. How good it felt to be loved. How good it felt to be going home.

When they got back to the farm, Hattie told each hen she was sorry for the way she had acted and for the unkind things she had said. The other hens soon forgave her. What a happy group they were that night when they flew up into the old tree.

As everyone was going to sleep, Hattie sang,

"I'm a small little hen, a plain little hen,
but a lucky hen am I.
I'm glad to be living with friends so forgiving
and a master who loves me nearby."

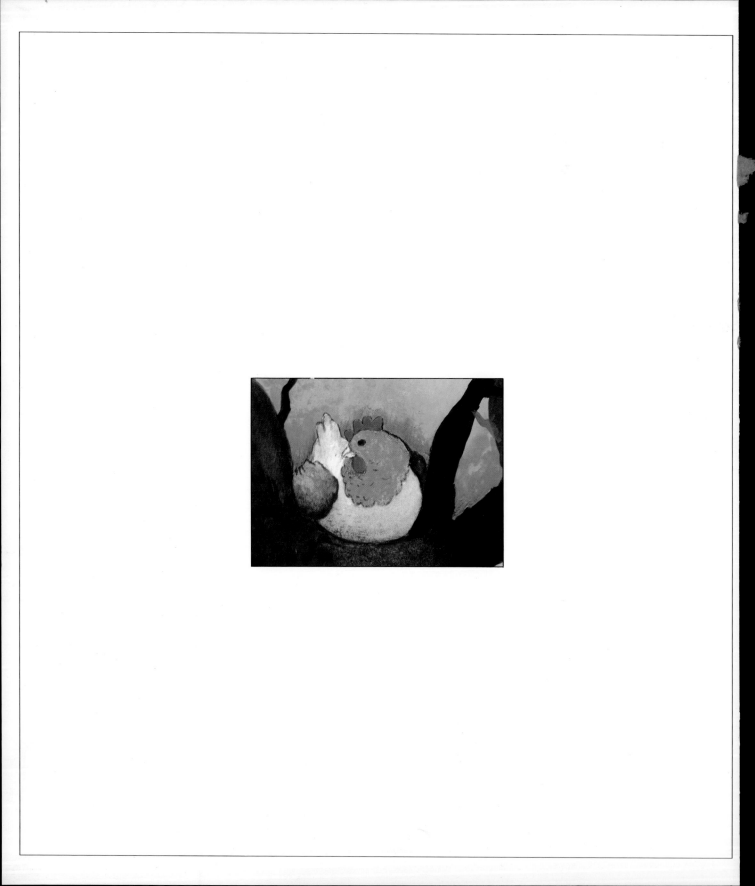